LIQUID COURAGE

ATTACK OF THE DELIRIUM TREMENS

Cover & Title Page Illustration by
Meesimo

Back Cover Illustrated by
Carlos Gabriel Ruiz

Colored by
Benjamin Sawyer

Edited by
Jason Green and Steve Higgins

Art Direction and Design by
Carlos Gabriel Ruiz

Some Fonts Provided by Nate Piekos & Blambot

Special Thanks to Schlafly & the
Schlafly Bottleworks in Maplewood, MO

LIQUID COURAGE II: ATTACK OF THE DELIRIUM TREMENS
ISBN 978-1-948079-02-0

Zero to Hero

by Jonathan J. Norfleet   Illustration by John King

Do you remember your introduction to superheroes? And I'm not talking about your first comic strip or floppy or whatever. Forget about that for now; I'm talking about your first exposure. I'd wager that it's unlikely that you do, not because your memory is bad, but simply that superheroes have been such a large part of our collective cultural zeitgeist for so long, it's likely that they have simply been with you your entire life: through clothing, movies, radio, graffiti, catchphrases, etc. And as we fast-forward to today, it is very clear that superheroes will never leave us. They continue to be all around us which, quite frankly, is fantastic. Or incredible. Or amazing. Or uncanny. Or... well, you get the picture.

So here we are, *Liquid Courage II* has finally arrived. It's been 8 years since the release of the first superhero anthology from Ink and Drink Comics. And if I'm remembering correctly, it was the largest overall effort from the collective. I, myself, contributed to that book, writing and penciling a story that I intentionally saddled with the longest title in the anthology. It was about a brave space knight getting his butt kicked for the entire length of the story by a Space Amazonian wrestler inspired by the Ultimate Warrior. Sometimes heroes lose. And at face value, that's all it was. But on the meta level, it was an attempt at dropping the reader into the middle of a story arc with no explanation outside of the title, to take them on a ride as our hero struggles to communicate to his opponent, as she clotheslines and suplexes him into oblivion in the ancient ruins of some far-off planet.

Now, when I started this introduction, I brought up the idea of our first exposure to superheroes, while explicitly telling you to not focus on your first superhero comic. If you did think about that, it's likely that your first superhero comic wasn't a #1 first appearance of the titular character, but instead, it was some random issue of some series that had been running for years even decades before you were born. And my attempt with my story was to recreate that feeling: a story already in progress, but that was simple enough to follow and understand the nature of the events within. And perhaps it would entice the reader to want more. (This was also an attempt to backdoor a much larger effort with those characters for an independent venture, but that's a story for another day.)

So why am I talking about a story that has nothing to do with this current collection? Well, I guess this anecdote really just ties in with the nature of these anthologies. They exist for creatives to experiment with short-form storytelling in any given genre, to be able to challenge themselves and the readers to a concept that can be an attention grabber and leave a lasting impression. Because at the end of the day, functional comics are hard work. For some, they are simply a hobby. For others? It is their career, their life, their legacy. Wherever someone falls in the scheme of comics, it takes a lot for someone to put their work out there to be consumed by the masses. Some would call that "courage"... and for creating a new superhero in a world already full to the brim with superheroes, perhaps that involves a little bit of liquid courage... too. Two.

Liquid Courage II.

See what I did there? That's right, folks; I spent this whole introduction as a means to craft a title drop pun. I won't be apologizing for that. But I do hope you enjoy the stories within the pages of this book. It's been a long time coming. Because while superheroes may truly be a dime a dozen these days, that doesn't mean that there isn't always room for more.

- Jonathan J. Norfleet

A guy who has found yet another way to talk about his own past contributions in the introduction of a new book.

When last we saw CAPTAIN COURAGE, he was facing off against that denizen of darkness THE BLUE HORROR. The vindictive villain had designs on destroying the corporate headquarters of his former employer SAUNDERS and SUTTON Inc. Our hero succeeded in preventing this preposterous plot, only to discover that two of his greatest nemeses had joined forces! THE BLUE HORROR was being assisted by the magical malcontent DELIRIA! Her scandalous sorcery had transmogrified the minions in THE BLUE HORROR's thrall into the terrible DELIRIUM TREMORS! The captured captain is in their clutches at this very moment, as we continue our story for the thrilling conclusion of...

GOING OFF THE FURROW!

STRUGGLE AS YOU MIGHT BUT YOU WILL NEVER BREAK FREE! I'VE FINALLY BEATEN YOU, CAPTAIN COURAGE!

I MUST ESCAPE BEFORE HIS DEATH-RAY ACTIVATES!

PENNED BY STEVE HIGGINS, ILLUSTRATED BY MEESIMO

WITH YOU GONE, I CAN FINALLY GET REVENGE ON THOSE WHO HAVE WRONGED ME!

"ONCE I WAS A FOOLISH DRONE WORKING FOR A COMPANY I LOVED. BUT I SHOULD HAVE KNOWN A CORPORATION COULD NEVER TRULY CARE ABOUT THEIR EMPLOYEES!

STEAD THEY CUT CORNERS N SAFETY PRECAUTIONS TO SAVE MONEY, ND I WAS THEIR HAPLESS VICTIM!

THE INDUSTRIAL ACCIDENT LEFT ME *HORRIBLY* DEFORMED, FORCING ME TO SEEK THE DARKNESS AND SHUN THE LIGHT.

ERE I MET THE ORK-ORKS, EWER-DWELLING CREATURES WITH HEIR OWN FUNCTIONING SOCIETY BUT THOUT A LEADER TO GUIDE THEM!

SO I TOOK CHARGE, LEADING THEM IN THEIR QUEST TO COME UP INTO THE WORLD DENIED TO THEM...

...AND AVENGE THEMSELVES ON THOSE ABOVE THE CLAY.

MUST KEEP HIM DISTRACTED...

BUT THAT'S NOT HOW IT HAPPENED! YOU WERE DRUNK ON THE JOB!

BVMP!

THERE WAS NO ONE TO BLAME FOR THAT ACCIDENT BUT YOURSELF!

THE ORK-ORKS WERE PERFECTLY HAPPY UNDERGROUND...

LIVING IN A SOCIALIST UTOPIA AND PERFECTLY WELCOMING IN NATURE...

...UNTIL YOU CAME ALONG AND ESTABLISHED YOURSELF AS A DESPOTIC TYRANT!

AND YOUR "DEFORMITY?" BARELY A SCRATCH! IT ACTUALLY KINDA MAKES YOU LOOK TOUGH...

And remember, kids:
never drink while on the job!

The Savage DAN AMMO IN "OUT OF RETIREMENT"

STORY, ART AND WORDS BY BARRY LINCOLN

BEFORE HE BECAME THE **LEGENDARY** AMERICAN HERO, DAN WORKED FOR THE U.S. GOVERNMENT AS A CLERK. HIS TASK WAS THE ORGANIZATION OF DECADE-OLD TAX RETURNS.

WITH HIS FRAIL, PUNY SKIN, HIS GREATEST **THREAT** WAS A PAPERCUT.

IN THE LAB DEPARTMENT OF THAT BUILDING, A **SECRET** TECHNICAL/ BIOLOGICAL HYBRID BOMB ACCIDENTALLY DETONATED.

EVERYONE IN THE UPPER WING WAS KILLED IN THE EXPLOSION.

EVERYONE **EXCEPT** DAN.

UNEXPLAINABLY, THE EFFECTS OF THE BOMB **MUTATED** DAN'S DNA. THIS MUTATION BESTOWED DAN WITH SUPER STRENGTH AND INVULNERABILITY.

ALONG WITH THE MUTATION, HIS BODY GAINED **MASSIVE** MUSCLE DENSITY.

NO LONGER WEAK, THE GOVERNMENT SAW DAN AS AN **OPPORTUNITY**.

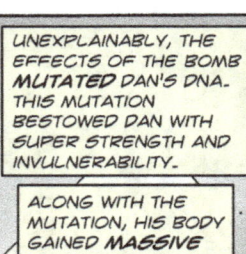

DAN BECAME THE TOP FIELD AGENT AND FOILED **COUNTLESS** EVILS THAT THREATENED AMERICA.

HE IS **DAN AMMO!**

DAN AMMO BECAME AMERICA'S **SUPERHERO**.

YEARS INTO HIS CAREER, DAN STARTED A FAMILY.

UNFORTUNATELY, THIS WASN'T THE HAPPY ENDING HE DESERVED.

THERE WAS ONE OTHER SURVIVOR IN THE EXPLOSION, AND HE BLAMED DAN FOR HIS PHYSICAL PREDICAMENT. HIS NAME IS **DOCTOR EDWARD QUIETUS**.

DR. QUIETUS SOUGHT REVENGE, **KILLING** DAN'S WIFE.

ENRAGED, DAN WENT AFTER DR. QUIETUS. AND AFTER A BATTLE OF **REVENGES**, DAN EMERGED TRIUMPHANT.

A BITTERSWEET ENDING FOR DAN.

WITH HIS SPIRIT BROKEN, DAN WENT INTO SECLUSION. HE RETIRED FROM BEING AMERICA'S **SUPERHERO**.

OVER THE YEARS, THE STORY OF **DAN AMMO** BECAME THAT OF LEGEND.

THEN LEGEND BECAME **MYTH**.

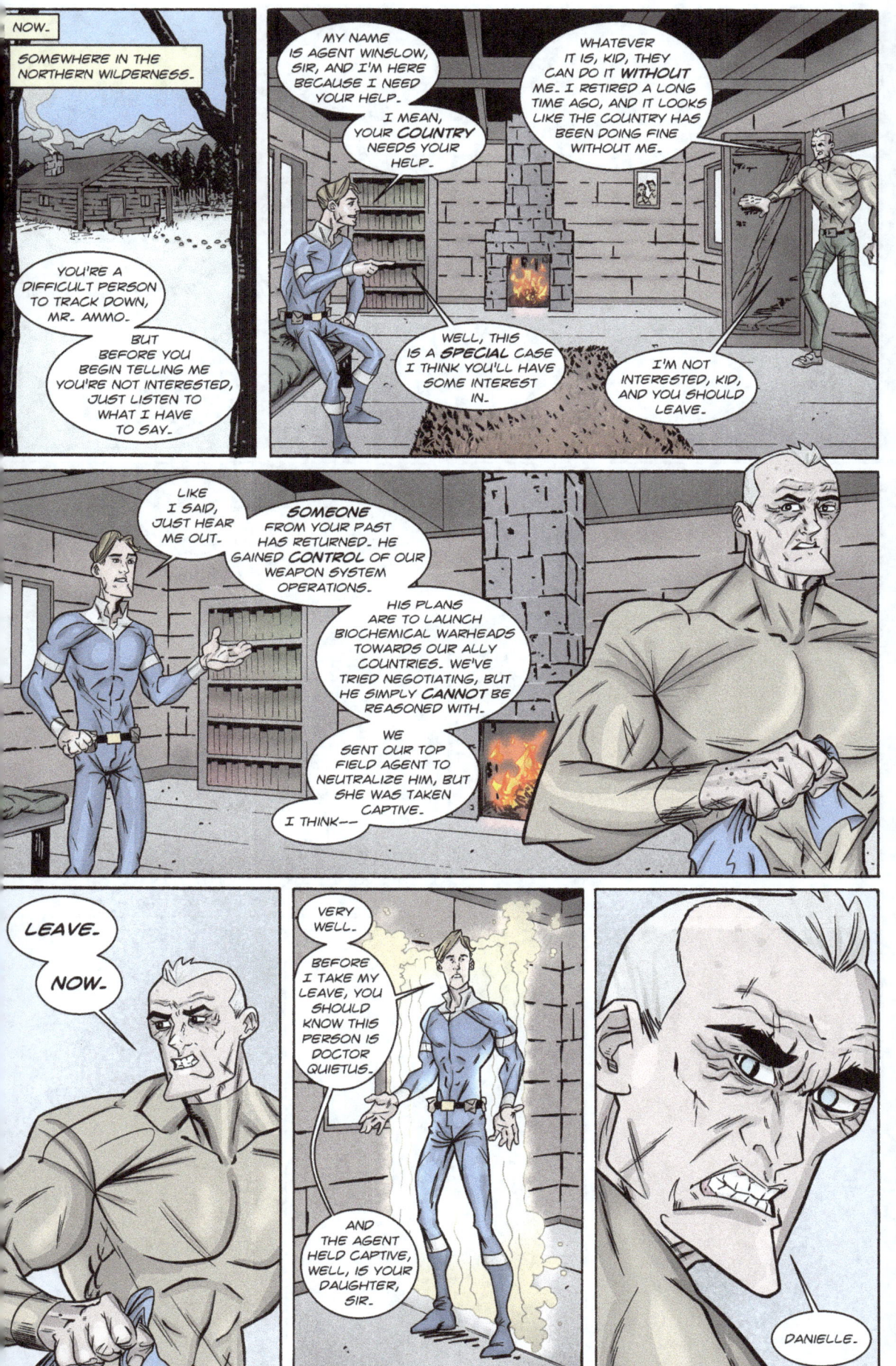

NOW.

SOMEWHERE IN THE NORTHERN WILDERNESS.

YOU'RE A DIFFICULT PERSON TO TRACK DOWN, MR. AMMO.

BUT BEFORE YOU BEGIN TELLING ME YOU'RE NOT INTERESTED, JUST LISTEN TO WHAT I HAVE TO SAY.

MY NAME IS AGENT WINSLOW, SIR, AND I'M HERE BECAUSE I NEED YOUR HELP.

I MEAN, YOUR COUNTRY NEEDS YOUR HELP.

WHATEVER IT IS, KID, THEY CAN DO IT WITHOUT ME. I RETIRED A LONG TIME AGO, AND IT LOOKS LIKE THE COUNTRY HAS BEEN DOING FINE WITHOUT ME.

WELL, THIS IS A SPECIAL CASE I THINK YOU'LL HAVE SOME INTEREST IN.

I'M NOT INTERESTED, KID, AND YOU SHOULD LEAVE.

LIKE I SAID, JUST HEAR ME OUT.

SOMEONE FROM YOUR PAST HAS RETURNED. HE GAINED CONTROL OF OUR WEAPON SYSTEM OPERATIONS.

HIS PLANS ARE TO LAUNCH BIOCHEMICAL WARHEADS TOWARDS OUR ALLY COUNTRIES. WE'VE TRIED NEGOTIATING, BUT HE SIMPLY CANNOT BE REASONED WITH.

WE SENT OUR TOP FIELD AGENT TO NEUTRALIZE HIM, BUT SHE WAS TAKEN CAPTIVE.

I THINK--

LEAVE.

NOW.

VERY WELL.

BEFORE I TAKE MY LEAVE, YOU SHOULD KNOW THIS PERSON IS DOCTOR QUIETUS.

AND THE AGENT HELD CAPTIVE, WELL, IS YOUR DAUGHTER, SIR.

DANIELLE.

ALL RIGHT, LADIES, LISTEN UP. STEALTH IS **KEY** FOR THIS MISSION. YOUR OBJECTIVE IS PARACHUTING INSIDE THE COMPOUND.

ONCE INSIDE, YOU WILL COVER MR. AMMO AS HE NEUTRALIZES THE TARGET.

I CAN'T BELIEVE YOU'RE REAL! YOU'RE, LIKE, A TOTAL LEGEND!

HEARING YOUR STORIES INSPIRED ME TO JOIN THE FORCE! I CANNOT BELIEVE I'M GOING ON A MISSION WITH **THE** DAN AMMO!

LET'S MOVE IT TEAM!

WHERE'S YOUR PARACHUTE, SIR?!

HRM.

WRRKOOM

THREE LITTLE BIRDS.

AND ONE LONE WOLF.

BLAM

BLAM

BLAM

TNK

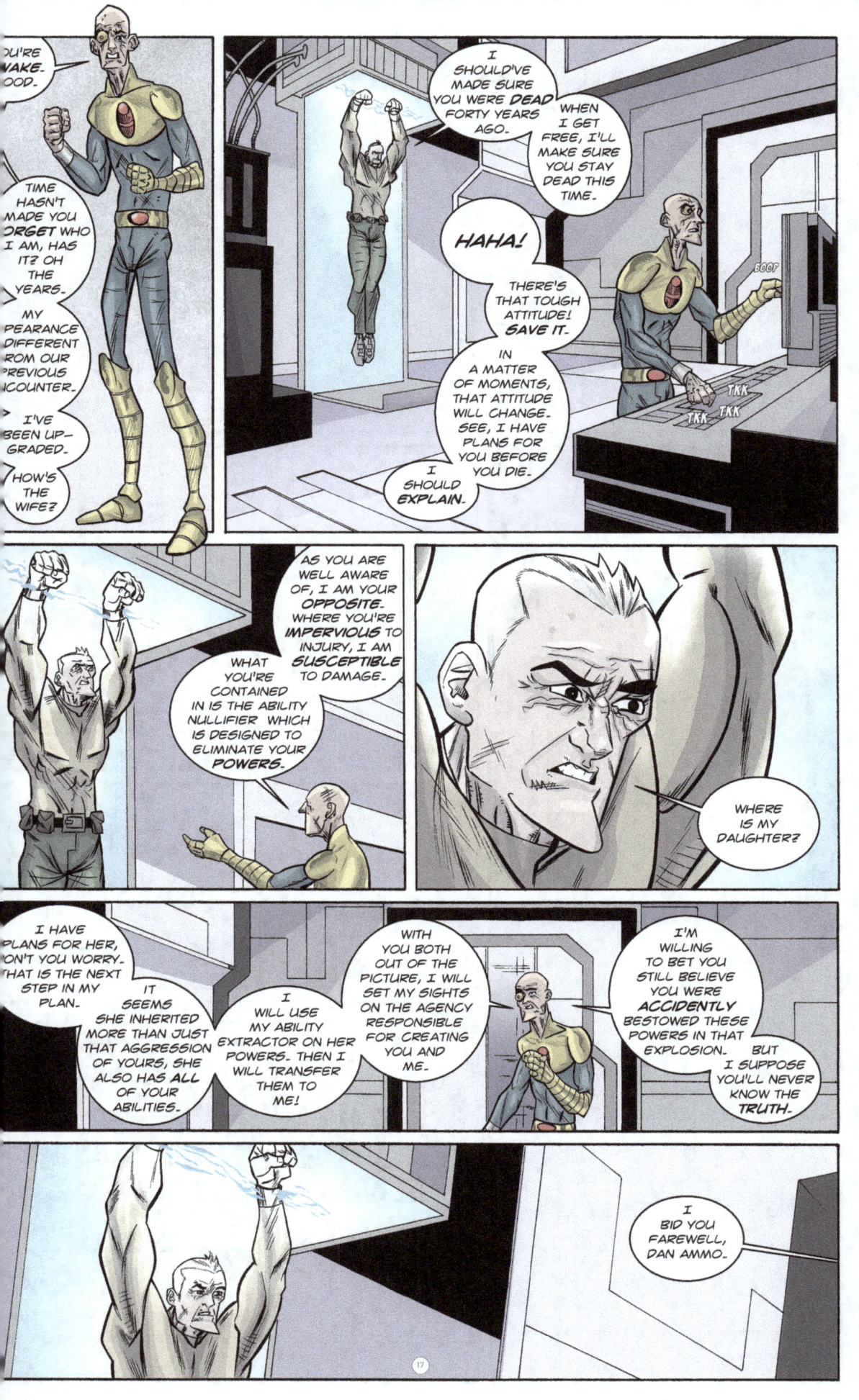

PTOO

CLK

BZZRTT

HRM... WHERE ARE THE WEAPONS?

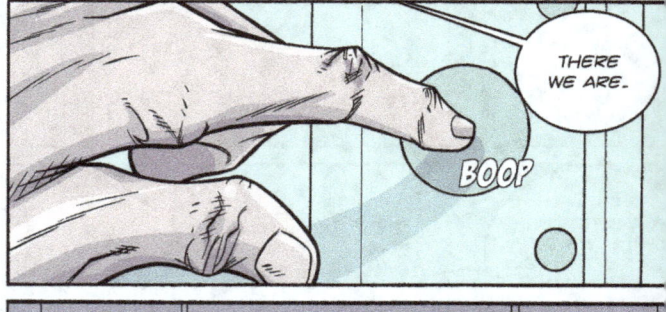

THERE WE ARE...

BOOP

TIME TO *FINISH* THIS SO I CAN ENJOY MY RETIRE— MENT.

18

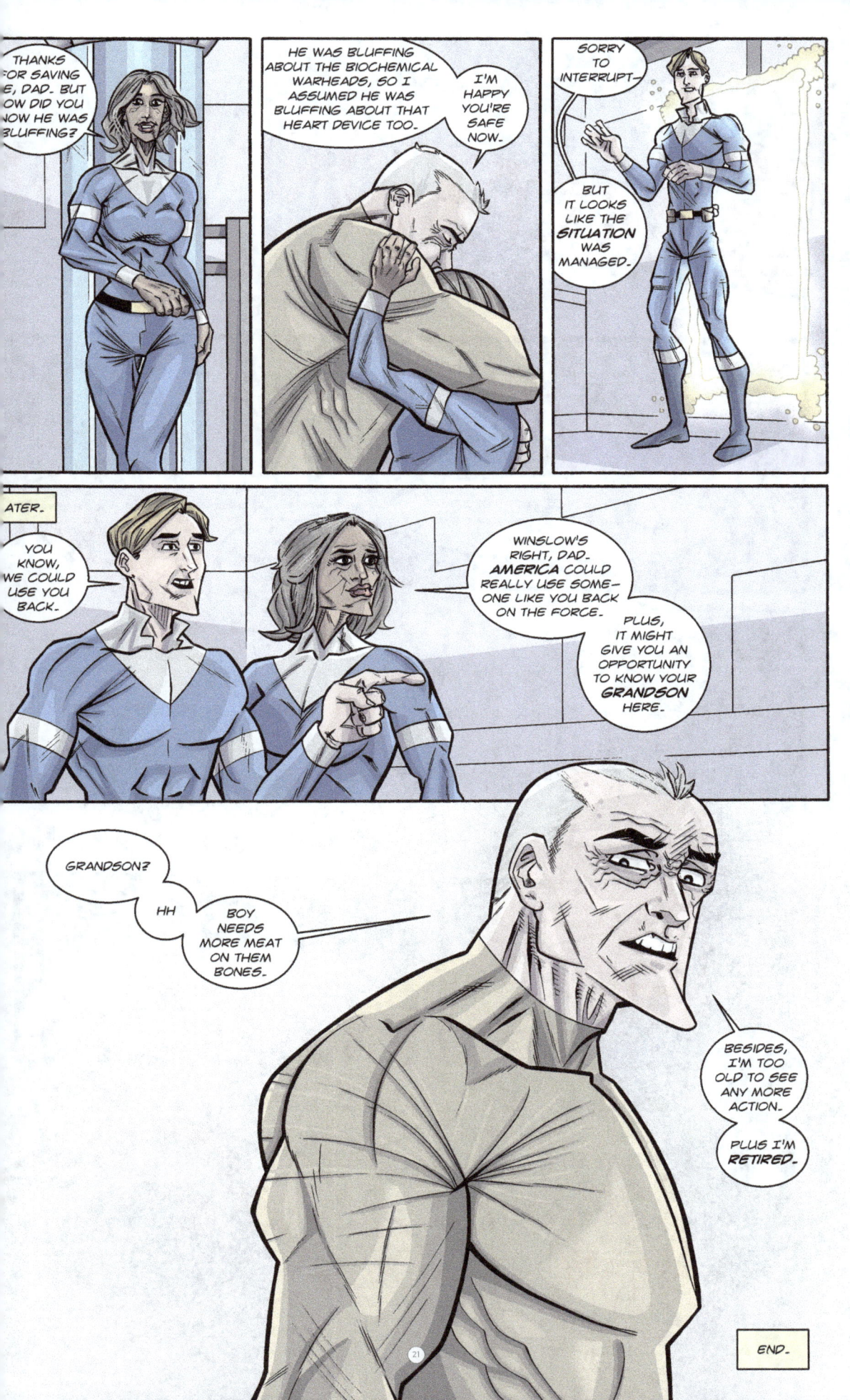

THANKS FOR SAVING ~E, DAD. BUT ~OW DID YOU ~NOW HE WAS ~LUFFING?

HE WAS BLUFFING ABOUT THE BIOCHEMICAL WARHEADS, SO I ASSUMED HE WAS BLUFFING ABOUT THAT HEART DEVICE TOO.

I'M HAPPY YOU'RE SAFE NOW.

SORRY TO INTERRUPT—

BUT IT LOOKS LIKE THE SITUATION WAS MANAGED.

~ATER.

YOU KNOW, ~WE COULD USE YOU BACK.

WINSLOW'S RIGHT, DAD. AMERICA COULD REALLY USE SOMEONE LIKE YOU BACK ON THE FORCE.

PLUS, IT MIGHT GIVE YOU AN OPPORTUNITY TO KNOW YOUR GRANDSON HERE.

GRANDSON?

HH

BOY NEEDS MORE MEAT ON THEM BONES.

BESIDES, I'M TOO OLD TO SEE ANY MORE ACTION.

PLUS I'M RETIRED.

END.

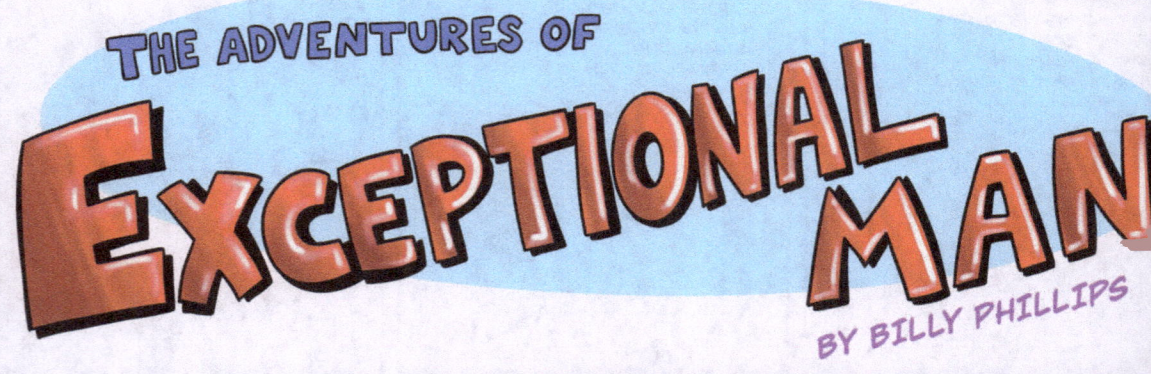

THE ADVENTURES OF EXCEPTIONAL MAN

BY BILLY PHILLIPS

I THOUGHT YOU WOULD HAVE LEFT FOR WORK BY NOW.

THAT WAS THE PLAN, BUT THEN OUR CAT CLIMBED UP INTO THE CAR AND I CAN'T GET HER OUT.

WHAT ARE WE GOING TO DO?

I SENSED TROUBLE. HOW CAN I HELP?

HERE COMES, EXCEPTIONAL MAN! PERHAPS, HE CAN HELP.

OH, CRAP.

OUR CAT CLIMBED UP INTO MY CAR'S ENGINE.

DON'T WORRY. I CAN RETRIEVE YOUR CAT!

HERE, KITTY, KITTY, KITTY!

SAVED THE DAY, AGAIN!

HERE YOU GO!

GUESS I NEED TO CALL WORK AND LET THEM KNOW I'LL BE LATE.

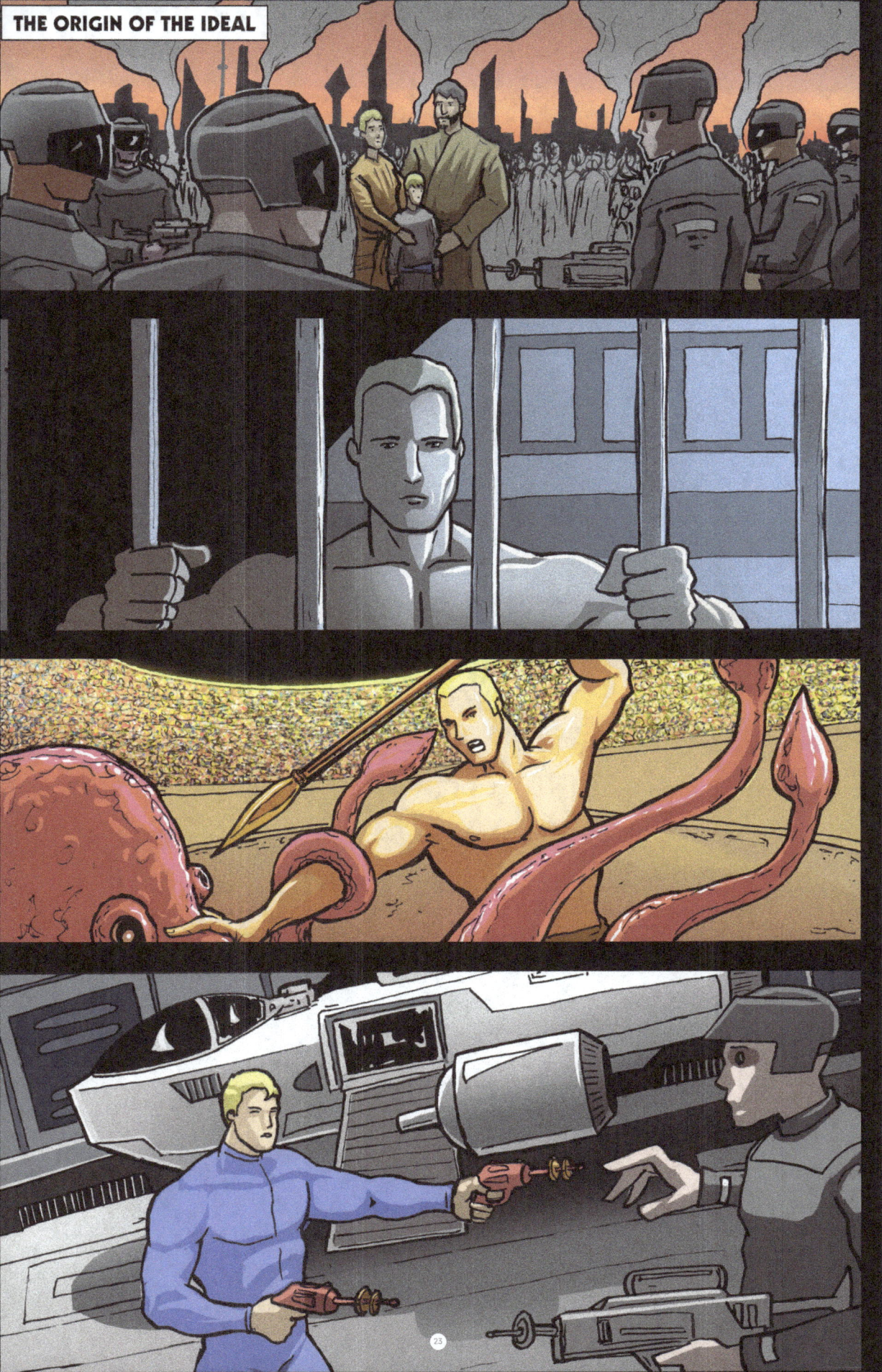

EVERYBODY'S FAVORITE SUPERHERO
THE IDEAL

IN
WHAT COST A HERO?

WRITTEN & ILLUSTRATED BY
CARLOS GABRIEL RUIZ

COLORED BY
BENJAMIN SAWYER

ECONOMISTS ACROSS THE GLOBE ARE CONCERNED ABOUT AN IMPENDING RECESSION THAT COULD HAVE DEVASTATING EFFECTS TO THE WORLD MARKETS.

BREAKING NEWS -- FLIGHT 2203 FROM CHICAGO TO METRO CITY EXPERIENCED SOME ABNORMAL ENGINE TROUBLES WHEN A FLOCK OF SEAGULLS RAN INTO THE PLANE AS IT WAS STARTING ITS DESCENT TO METRO CITY INTERNATIONAL AIRPORT.

AGAINST ALL EXPECTATIONS, THE MOVIE IS A SURPRISE HIT AMID A FRIGID ENTERTAINMENT CLIMATE.

WAS HE BORN WITH THOSE EXTRAORDINARY POWERS, OR DID SOME FREAK GAMMA BOMB ACCIDENT CAUSE HIM TO GAIN HIS SUPERHUMAN STRENGTH?

IS HE AN ALIEN HIDING AMONGST US HUMANS?

DOES IT REALLY MATTER? SHOULDN'T ALL THE GOOD HE DOES ON A DAILY BASIS BE ENOUGH TO PACIFY OUR FEARS?

WHAT ELSE DOES HE NEED TO DO FOR EVERYONE TO BELIEVE?

A NEW PLAGUE? SCIENTISTS IN ASIA HAVE DISCOVERED MOSQUITO **11:15PM ET**

ULTIMATE POWER! IMAGINE THAT. THE IDEAL IS A BEING -- BECAUSE, LET'S FACE IT, WE'RE NOT SURE IF HE'S EVEN HUMAN -- THAT CAN DO ANYTHING IN THE WORLD. TO ANYONE. AT ANY TIME. AND WE ARE POWERLESS TO STOP HIM.

SOME PEOPLE THINK THAT HE IS MANKIND'S SAVIOR, BUT I THINK HE'S MORE LIKE OUR DEMISE. HE'S WAITING FOR THE RIGHT MOMENT TO STEP IN AND TAKE OVER THE EARTH, AND WE'RE PRETTY MUCH LETTING HIM!

THE IDEAL SCENARIO FOR *US* IS WORLD *WITHOUT HIM*.

10:15 CT

Is your data safe? Hackers have just unlocked your cell phone!

PFE 30.50 ⌃   DD 63.83 ⌃   NKE 60.08 ⌃   UNH 125.10 ⌃   GE 30.34 ⌃   IBM 142.36 ⌃   V 71.63

WHAT ARE THEY MEETING ABOUT, KEVIN? ARE THEY GOING TO DEBATE HOW BAD THE WORLD IS WITHOUT HIM? I THINK HE'S PRETTY MUCH THE IDEAL SUPERHERO!

I SEE WHAT YOU DID THERE, BARB, AND I'M NOT IMPRESSED. I THINK YOU JUST LIKE THE WAY HIS TIGHTS CLING TO HIM.

I CAN'T ARGUE WITH YOU THERE, KEV.

ENTERTAINMENT NEWS CABLE CHANNEL   8:15PM PT

QB Jimmy Stone was spotted in Las Vegas with a dozen strippers a

MMmMMmmph!!!
PLEH!
HEY, IS SOMEBODY WALKING BY OUT THERE?
I SAW THE HALLWAY LIGHTS ACTIVATE.
PLEASE...
OH, THANK GOD.
I DIDN'T. I'M TRAPPED! TIED UP AND STUFF.
CAN YOU FIND A WAY TO GET IN?
HOW DID YOU ATTACH THIS PADLOCK FROM THE INSIDE, MAN?
UH...HANG ON.

TURN YOUR HEAD!
HEH!
HAIL MARY, FULL OF--
AAHHH-
CHOOOOOOOOOO!!!
I'M SO SORRY.
TSSSSSSSS
TSSSSSSSSSSS

ELMHURST: A PRETTY NAME FOR A NEIGHBORHOOD WHOSE RICH FOREST WAS LONG AGO REPLACED BY CONCRETE AND GLASS. THE WHOLE CITY IS NOW A WASTELAND, BUT ELMURST IS THE WORST OF THE WORST. STILL, SCAVENGERS LIKE MIKE AND TAMMY HEAR TALES OF WAREHOUSES STILL BRIMMING WITH SUPPLIES AND THEY COME TO SCAVENGE. THEY HEAR RUMORS OF *THE HELLIONS*, THE BEASTS THAT GUARD THESE BARREN STREETS.

GRR...FOOLISH HUMANS!

BY THE TIME THEY FIND OUT THOSE RUMORS ARE *TRUE*, IT'S ALREADY TOO LATE.

THE HELLIONS. I--I CAN'T BELIEVE THEY'RE REAL!

DEAR GOD--!

HAHAHA HAHA!!! YOUR GOD HAS NO PLACE HERE!

TAMMY, *RUN.* RUN AS FAST AS YOU CAN AND DON'T LOOK BACK.

BUT MIKE, I JUST CAN'T!

YOU HAVE TO. I LOVE YOU.

I LOVE YOU, TOO. I'LL HOLD THEM OFF AS LONG AS I CAN.

THE BEAST'S SCREECH FEELS LIKE A KNIFE PIERCING MIKE'S SKULL. EVEN AT A DISTANCE, HE CAN FEEL THE HEAT OF ITS BREATH. HE WATCHES AS IF IN SLOW MOTION AS ITS SHARP CLAWS AND FANGS COME EVER CLOSER, HIS BULLETS HARMLESSLY RICOCHETING OFF ITS HIDE. HIS LIFE FLASHES BEFORE HIS EYES.

THEN, SUDDENLY, HE SEES A VERY DIFFERENT KIND OF "FLASH."

THE HELLION COLLAPSES TO THE GROUND, ALREADY DEAD. MIKE'S MIND RUNS A MILE A MINUTE. A STRAY THOUGHT ENTERS: IT SMELLS EVEN WORSE WHILE IT'S *COOKING*.

THE REMAINING HELLIONS FLEE.

WHO-- WHO *DID* THIS?!

HE'S AFRAID OF THE ANSWER.

HE TURNS TO SEE THREE FIGURES. THAT TWO OF THEM SEEM HUMANOID OFFERS LITTLE COMFORT CONSIDERING THE APPEARANCE OF THE *THIRD*.

HEY, MAN. YOU OKAY? YOU'RE CRAZY TO COME DOWN HERE WITH JUST THAT PEASHOOTER. YOU'RE JUST LUCKY *AMMON* SPOTTED YOU.

AMMON.

...AND THAT I DECIDED TO WASTE MY *HELLFIRE* ON SOMEONE SO *STUPID*.

STOP IT, AMMON, YOU'LL SCARE HIM! HI, WE'RE FROM...

I KNOW WHO YOU ARE. YOU'RE FROM *THE HOPE CORPORATION*. YOU SAVED ME JUST SO YOU COULD STEAL ME FOR YOUR EXPERIMENTS.

BLAST.

NIGHTFALL.

WELL, I'M NOT GOING DOWN WITHOUT A *FIGHT!*

I THINK YU'VE GOT THE WRONG IDEA.

WHAT-- WHAT *ARE* YOU?!

THE HOPE CORPORATION CONTROLS THIS LAND, BUT THEY DON'T EXPERIMENT ON ANYONE.

WHAT THEY'RE HIDING IS A LITERAL PORTAL TO *HELL*.

THE HELLIONS YOU SAW COME FROM THE OTHER SIDE.

THEY PROTECT THE PORTAL FOR HOPE IN EXCHANGE FOR THEIR FREEDOM. THEY ATTACK ANYONE WHO ENTERS ELMHURST.

AND THAT'S WHERE WE COME IN. WE KILL EVERY ONE OF THOSE BASTARD HELLIONS WE COME ACROSS.

OUR ULTIMATE MISSION IS TO DESTROY OR PUSH BACK ALL OF THE HELLIONS AND RESEAL THE PORTAL. WE'RE THE ARMY FIGHTING FOR THE FREEDOM OF EVERYONE IN THIS *DAMNED NATION*.

WE OPERATE IN SECRET, DESTROYING HELLIONS FROM THE SHADOWS. DO NOT BREATHE A **WORD** OF WHAT YOU SAW HERE TODAY!

DON'T WORRY! YOUR SECRET IS SAFE WITH ME. I'M--I'M JUST GLAD SOMEONE IS FIGHTING THIS FIGHT.

RETURN VIA THE ROUTE YOU TOOK IN. IT SHOULD BE SAFE NOW, BUT MOVE QUICKLY, BEFORE THEY REGROUP.

I WILL. FAREWELL.

ANOTHER SCAVENGER FOUND AND SAVED. RESOURCES ARE GETTING SO SCARCE ON THE OUTSIDE--I WORRY SOON THERE WILL BE MORE THAN WE CAN EVER HOPE TO PROTECT.

THAT'S WHAT KEEPS ME UP AT NIGHT.

I KEEP TELLING **SEER** WE MUST MAKE LOCATING THE PORTAL A PRIORITY OVER THESE RESCUE MISSIONS.

AND WHAT? LET THESE INNOCENTS DIE?

IF IT MEANS CLOSING THE PORTAL SOONER AND SAVING MILLIONS IN THE PROCESS?

ABSOLUTELY.

PSSHT BLAST, REPORT.

THREE HELLIONS AMBUSHED TWO SCAVENGERS. WE GOT ONE BEAST BUT THE OTHER TWO ESCAPED.

DAMN! YOU MUST TRACK THEM DOWN!

IF THEY REACH THE **HELLION HIVE**, OUR PRESENCE WILL BE REVEALED!

SEER.

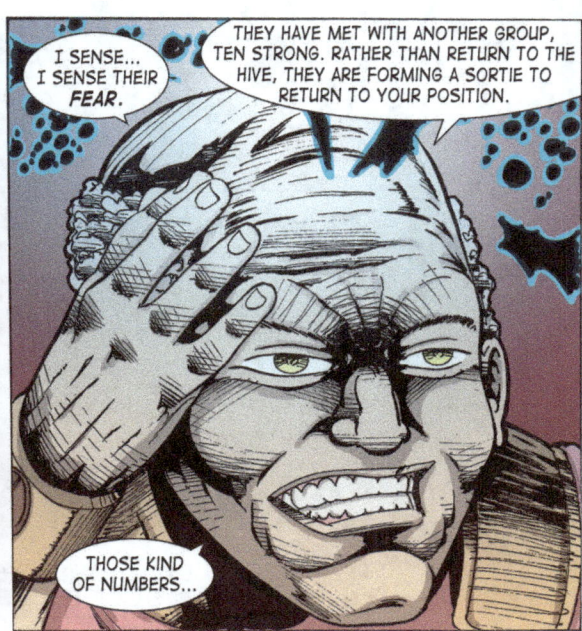

I SENSE... I SENSE THEIR **FEAR**.

THEY HAVE MET WITH ANOTHER GROUP, TEN STRONG. RATHER THAN RETURN TO THE HIVE, THEY ARE FORMING A SORTIE TO RETURN TO YOUR POSITION.

THOSE KIND OF NUMBERS...

DAMNED NATION
HARRINGTON-GREEN-ROACH

HAILSTONE.

HELL-BAT.

...CALL FOR **REINFORCEMENTS**.

THE END?

NightCity

DARKNESS FALLS.

STREETS AND ALLEYWAYS SHROUDED IN FEAR.

EVERY POST I SEE SHOWS SOCIETY DESCENDING FURTHER INTO CHAOS.

A WORLD UNSAFE FOR GOD-FEARING, LAW-ABIDING CITIZENS LIKE ME.

Writer & Artist Kevin Taylor

Colourist Jackie Rabbit

BUT NO MORE.

A TRUE HERO STANDS FOR WHAT HE *KNOWS* IS RIGHT!

AND HIS TIME IS NOW!

HEY KID!

...GET YOUR ASS BACK HERE!

S-STOP RIGHT THERE, OFFENDER!

SEE THE ERROR OF YOUR WAYS...

...OR GET A SLICE...

...OF JUSTICE!

THE ADVENTURES OF EXCEPTIONAL MAN

BY BILLY PHILLIPS

I'M HERE FOR MY FIRST EYE EXAM!

WELCOME, EXCEPTIONAL MAN! WE ARE HAPPY TO HAVE YOU. LET'S GET STARTED.

NOW, WE WILL DILATE YOUR EYES SO WE CAN...

BLAM

SQUALK

KABOOM

CRASH

WHAT'S HAPPENING TO ME!

CLOSE YOUR EYES, YOU MANIAC!

IS EVERYONE ALRIGHT?! DID I CAUSE ANY DAMAGE?!

THE INEXORABLE EXTREMITIES

SPIKE∘ MAX∘ SILK SIREN∘ WHAT A BUNCH OF *SHOW OFFS!*

DDLE MICS

25 US
75 CAN
268
JULY
2461

MEESIMO "AFTER" JIM LEE

SILK, BETTER LET ME TAKE LEAD ON THIS NEXT MISSION.

EXCUSE ME?!

MY BRUTE STRENGTH AND FIERCENESS WILL BE NEEDED.

CLEARLY, IT IS MY LEVELHEADEDNESS AND WIT THAT WILL BRING US VICTORY.

HAH, AS IF!

SPIKE.

WE JUST NOW HAD OUR BUTTS KICKED, DUE TO YOUR TEMPER.

THEY AMBUSHED US!

FIRST, LET'S COOL OUR HEADS AT HEADQUARTERS, GET THE REST OF THE TEAM...

THEN PERHAPS YOU WILL COME TO YOUR SENSES.

WHATEVER! WE NEED TO STRIKE NOW! REVENGE!

YOUR STRIKES ARE USELESS, IF THEY ARE NOT WELL PLANNED.

WELCOME BACK, KIDDOS.

HEY SILK. YOU GUYS OKAY?

DON'T WORRY GUYS, WE CAN BARELY TELL YOU HAVE YOUR TAILS BETWEEN YOUR LEGS WHEN YOU'RE FLYING.

MIT

...WINS!

YOU KNUCKLEHEADS. IF YOU DON'T KILL EACH OTHER, I GOT NEXT.

GRRR...

YOU MAY BE THE STRONGEST, MAX, BUT I AM THE FASTE—

5 MINUTES! MAN, THIS THING SMELLS LIKE SASQUATCH'S BUTT, AFTER FIELD-HOCKEY PRACTICE.

THANKS?!

THESE ARE MY TEAMMATES, WHOM I TRUST WITH MY LIFE...

READY?

LAST CHANCE TO GIVE UP!

HAVE YOU ALWAYS BEEN THIS TALL?

SIGH.

LESS THAN 5 MINUTES, EH?

HAVING SECOND THOUGHTS?

NO

ARE YOU?

DUDE!! WHAT THE HECK?!

WHAT? AW, NARDS!!

TIME?

UH, 44 SECONDS, HEH...

THANKS FOR THE "WARMUP".

WELP.

COOLER HEADS PREVAIL.

STORY & ART BY JOE WILLS | COLORS BY BEN SAWYER & JOE WILLS

KRA-THOOM

GUESS HE GOT BORED.

ONE CIVILIAN REMANING.

WILL YOU *FOCUS*! GO LOOK FOR CIVILIANS! THE INDICATOR SAYS THERE'S ONE LEFT.

THERE'S NO ONE ELSE *HERE*! MAYBE IT'S A GLITCH?

THE INDICATOR NEVER LIES. KEEP LOOKING, AND *HURRY*! NOT SURE HOW LONG I CAN HOLD THIS *SHIELD*.

WHEE°°°WHEE°°°
WHEE°°°WHEE°°°
WHEE°°°WHEE°°°
WHEE°°°WHEE°°°

AYE, MA'AM. RESTARTING "EARTH 2020".

SHALL I INITIATE THE C-19 PROTOCOL?

REDUCE OUTBREAK MATRIX, BUT INCREASE THE STRENGTH ON THE CELESTIAL WARLORD.

I'LL NOT HAVE WEAKLINGS IN *MY CORPS.*

NO! SSGT. REED, THERE'S NO WAY WE'RE DOING THAT A *FIFTH* TIME.

ONCE WAS *MORE THAN ENOUGH!* AS *TRAINING SUPERVISOR,* I--

AND AS *SENIOR DRILL INSTRUCTOR, I* DETERMINE HOW MANY TIMES I RUN *MY* CADETS THROUGH SIM TRIALS.

NO ONE HAS RUN EARTH 2020 MORE THAN TWICE. ESPECIALLY WITH C-19 PROTOCOL ENGAGED.

SGT. GRANT, IF YOU WISH TO LEAVE MY TEAM, FEEL FREE...

BUT KNOW THIS, ANYONE WHO QUITS *MY TEAM* WILL BE IMMEDIATELY PLACED ON *SECURITY DETAIL...*

...FOR THE *REMAINDER* OF THEIR TOUR HERE. *NO LIBERTIES. NO* PRIVILEGES. UNDERSTOOD?

UNDERSTOOD. RUN THE SIM.

RUN THE SIM. BUT SET IT TO *MAX.* WHEN THEY FAIL, SEND THE ASSESSMENT RESULTS-- FOR THE *BOTH* OF THEM.

END.

HE LEAPS VIGILANTLY THROUGH THE CITY, EYES PEELED FOR VILLAINS.

sigh...

YOU FUCKIN' IDIOT.

I COULD GO GET SOME EGGROLLS.

OR PICK A ROOFTOP AND BEAT OFF.

OR I MIGHT GO BACK AND SMOKE OUT WITH THAT GUY.

THE ONLY THING I'M LOOKING FOR...

IS A COMFY PLACE TO NAP.

YOU NEVER BOTHERED TO GIVE ME A SECRET IDENTITY, ASSHOLE.

THANKS TO YOU, I'M JUST A REALLY GOOD-LOOKING HOMELESS GUY.

OK, YOU CAN END THE STORY NOW...

AND FUCK OFF.

St. Patrick isn't a saint at all, but the hostile villain Hot Foot in disguise!

That's a stupid fuckin' name!

Time to step up this plan.

This should light the place up!

Stop the puns, for fuck's sake.

What're you doing?

Don't you dare end this shit on a cliffhanger, you son of a...

TO BE CONTINUED

The CATTLE Hand

BY Thomas Watson

KARATE POWERED DINO-FIGHTERS

PATRICK WECK & NATHAN KENKEL

ON A DARE, FOUR YOUNG KARATE STUDENTS SNUCK INTO THE OLD SCIENCE MUSEUM.

AFTER AWAKENING THE SPIRITS OF THE FOSSILS, THEY TRANSFORMED INTO THE KARATE POWERED DINO-FIGHTERS!

A METEOR COMING TOWARDS EARTH!

COME ON DINO-FIGHTERS!

CHOP

KARATE CHOP HARDER!

CHUCK (THE LEADER)

WE NEED TO STOP DR. DENIAL'S MACHINES!

ELVIS (THE MEAN ONE)

KICK!

SLASH

WE CAN'T LET THAT METEOR HIT THE EARTH!

ARETHA (THE GIRL ONE)

BUDDY (THE SMART ONE) NEWTON'S GHOST! IT'LL BE AN EXTINCTION EVENT!

PUNCH

WAVEGIRL VS. EVIL M

Story by Katelyn Higgins
Adapted by Elizabeth Schweitzer and Steve Higgins
Colors by Christian Meesey

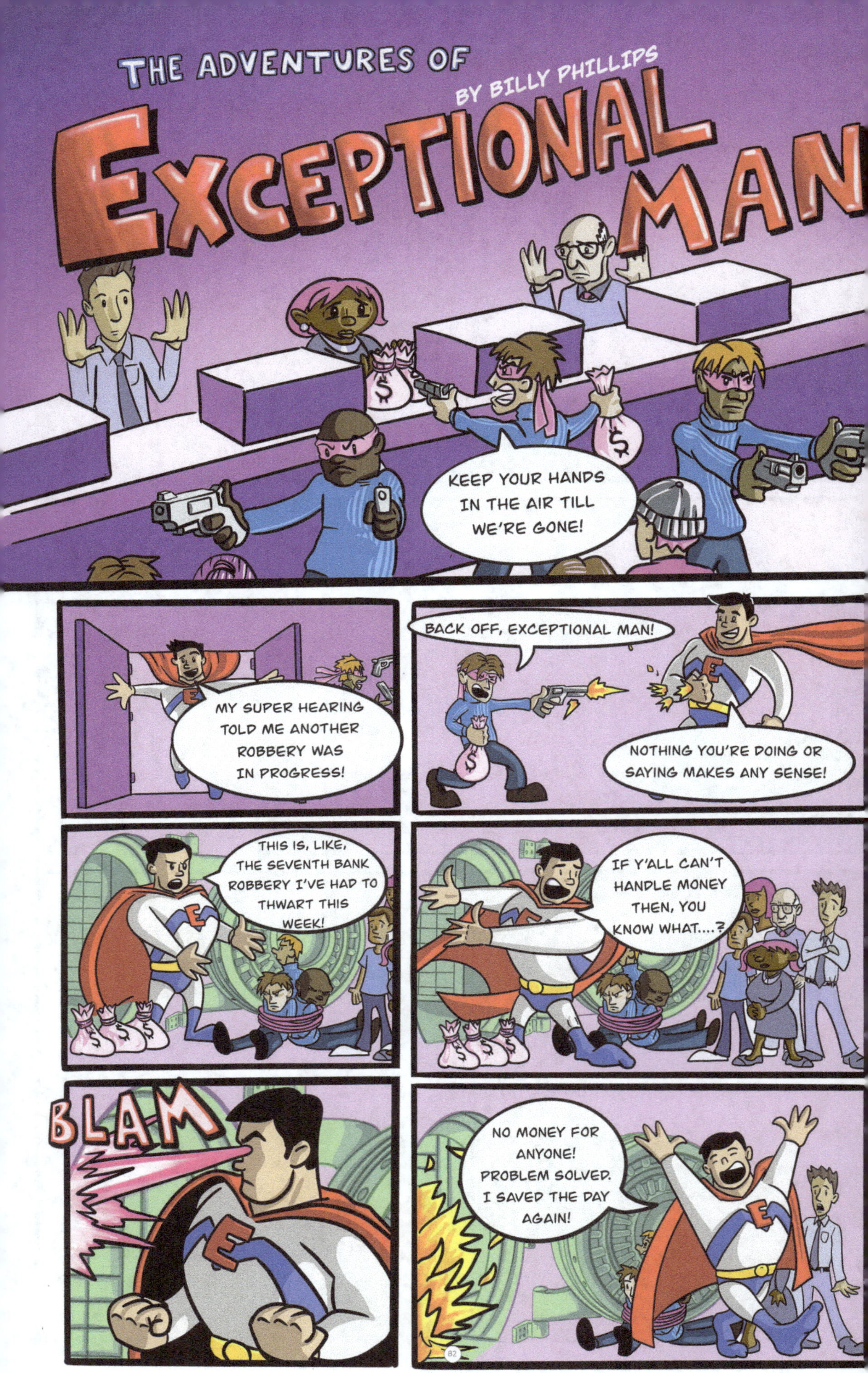

My hero

STORY:
RAGLIN
ART:
MEESIMO

FOR AS LONG AS I CAN REMEMBER... I'VE WANTED TO BE...

A SUPERHERO!

NOW:

I GET TO SHARE MY LOVE OF THEM...

...WITH HIM ➡

SEE THEM FOR THE FIRST TIME...

...ALL OVER AGAIN,

THROUGH HIS EYES.

USE THEIR STRENGTH,

TO HELP HIM...

WOBBLE

...FIND HIS OWN.

SUPERHEROES EMBODY OUR YEARNING FOR GREATNESS.

WHEEE,

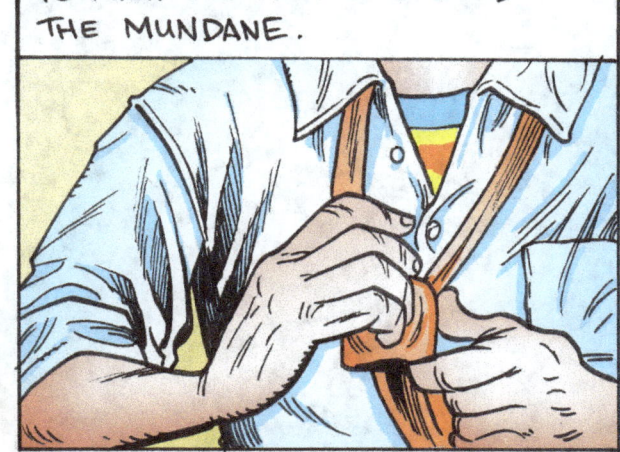

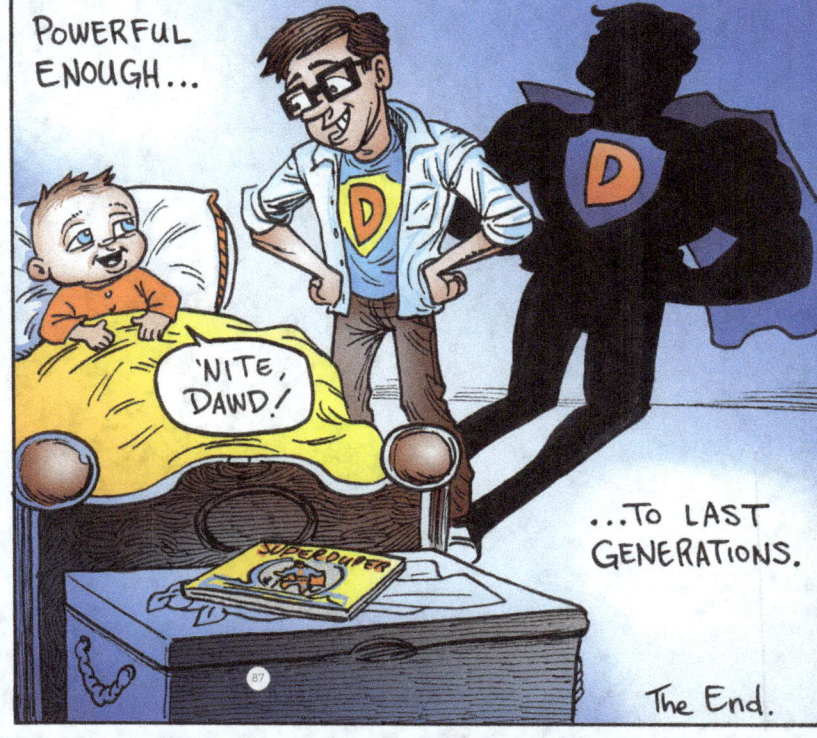

The End.

Daniel Scott Williams

1986-2022

Ink and Drink lost one of our own with the passing of D.S. Williams at the age of 36. As a writer, he contributed to several of our anthologies, including collaborations with his daughter F.J. Myles-Williams. But his passions went beyond comics, to his work as a musician, audio engineer, and prolific writer and producer of podcasts. His works can be found at iamdswilliams.com. He brought an inimitable sense of humor to our Ink and Drink meetings, and he will be missed. Rest In Peace.

Josh Barbeau

is a writer based out of St. Louis, MO, where he lives with his wife and three daughters. He is the creator of the fantasy-adventure comic series *Tyrants* and co-creator of the science fiction comic series *Earth A.M.*

Jason Green

is founder and Editor-In-Chief of **The Arts STL** (www.theartsstl.com), an arts-and-entertainment website based in St. Louis. His comics short stories have been collected in *Center of Gravity* (various artists) and *Collection* (with artist/co-writer Shawn Harrington), and he has published the first issue of *Sprawl*, a hyperviolent adventure set in a dystopian near-future St. Louis. He is the editor of the comics *Butcher Queen* and *The Atonement Bell* (both published by Red 5) and sci-fi novellas by Aaron Walther (the *Robot Pulp* series) and Nathan Kenkel (*Exogeny*).

Shawn Harrington

is an artist based in St. Louis. His previous published works appeared in the pages of the Ink and Drink anthologies *On the House 4th Round: Vampire Weekend, Juice Box, Sober, Spirits of St. Louis II: Hair of the Dog, Hungover: Stories from the Bottom of the Barrel*, and *Wasted*. He is currently working on a comic called *Bro Man*.

Katelyn Higgins

is an artist/person who writes random comics who lives in Florissant, Missouri with her dad Steve and her mom Sarah. In her free time, she draws animals, dragons, and Pokemon, occasionally failing at attempts to draw humans. She really loves cats. Wavegirl is her first published work featuring one of her OCs, and she's very grateful to Elizabeth for bringing the character to life.

Steve Higgins

is a professor of English at Lewis and Clark Community College. He has been a member of Ink and Drink Comics since it began in 2010, working as an editor/publisher for the group since 2012. He has released a collection of his early short comics entitled *Myriad Volume 1*, and he is currently at work on a second volume, as well as a collection of his fantasy stories with artist Christian (Meesimo) Meesey under the title *Katharos*. He resides in Florissant with his wife Sarah, his daughter Katelyn, and their brand new cat River. You can find him on Twitter, Instagram, and TikTok as @vacuumboy9.

Nathan Kenkel

is a reclusive writer from St. Louis, Missouri. He rarely leaves his house. When he does, it is only in the dark of night. No one has seen his face in twenty years, but rumors persist that it is pale and horrifying. As a rite of passage, neighborhood children dare the overgrown walkway leading to his front porch. None have reached the doorbell before fleeing back to the safety of their mothers. He has recently self-published *Exogeny*, a science-fiction novella under the pen name Nathan Karl.

John King

is an illustrator of comics hailing from the local St. Louis area. He has appeared in six Ink and Drink anthologies as well as three self-published books. He is a great appreciator of comic books and also enjoys building with Lego. To see his work, please visit johnkingart.deviantart.com or check his Instagram @johnkingillustrations.

Jesse Kwe

is a St. Louis transplant from North Carolina, but is also a lifelong artist. He loves drawing everything from dark, gritty horror to bright, colorful fairy tales. He worked on the Kickstarter-backed *Ghost Town* mini-series and has published a few other short stories in previous Ink and Drink anthologies. When he's not working or drawing, he's practicing martial arts or rehearsing his lines for theater. You can see more of his art on Instagram @jessekwe.

Barry Lincoln

grew up surrounded by cornfields and bordered by power lines, a typical mid-Illinoisan landscape. He took an interest in comics and art in his youth, publishing his first creator-owned superhero comic at the age of nine with the help of his mother's work's copy machine. He continuously seeks new ways to enhance his talents and aims to advance the quality of the stories he illustrates. If you're feeling adventurous, ask him about the multiverse and the concept of reality. His Instagram is @blincolnart.

Christian Meesey's

offbeat cartoons and caricatures have been displayed on walls and in rubbish bins worldwide for over 20 years! Meesey's work combines the foundational structure and methods of his mentors, Tom Richmond and C.F. Payne, with the sensibilities of early Image Comics as well as underground comic books. He is currently writing and/or illustrating *Time Shopper!* (with Tony Fleecs), *Ghost Agents* (with Rocko Jerome), *Turbo Hawk*, *Motley and Harv Meet a Dracula*, *Katharos* (with Steve Higgins) and various Ink and Drink anthologies. Meesey is a member of the National Cartoonists Society. He lives and draws somewhere in the Midwest.

Steve Meesey

is a St. Louis artist and lifelong art lover. You can find him on Instagram @f.c.field.

Jonathan J. Norfleet

wrote the intro to this book.

Billy Phillips

is an artist, illustrator and art teacher who currently lives in Sioux Falls, South Dakota. He's been drawing and making art his whole life and has shared the joy of creating with elementary and middle school students for over fifteen years. He uses his art to highlight wonder, joy, imagination, and the delightfully absurd. He's written and illustrated a few short comics, and he looks forward to doing more! You can view his current work on Instagram @sfumato07 and at billyphillipsart.com or www.facebook.com/billyphillipsart/.

Jackie Rabbit

is a published commercial artist and painter. She lives in a creepy old house in the woods with her partner and several wild beasts. To see more art and the occasional creature, follow her on Instagram @jackie_rabbit.

Chris Raglin

loves creating comics with his family and friends. His wife and two children are his greatest inspiration and the subject of most his work. You can follow his infrequent posts on instagram @chrisRraglin.

Bradley Roach

has spent decades traversing digital worlds, slaying dragons, raising the dead, and shattering ALL the pixels in an attempt to find all the colors in which one could illustrate the greatest stories ever told. Now his flask is full, his DKP towering, and his hands IRL are ready to unleash hell in all the prettiest of colors. You can follow his adventures on Instagram @skeletonhands or find him hanging out and sacrificing plants for consumption at his latest creation, a fortress of horror, metal, and tacos; Terror Tacos.

Carlos Gabriel Ruiz

is an award-winning writer, illustrator, and designer. He created the graphic novels *Pretentious Record Store Guy* and *Shorts + Losses*, the superhero comic *The Ideal*, and is the co-creator of the action-packed crime thriller *Blood on the Tracks* with Brian Atkins. He was a finalist in the Scriptapalooza Television Writing Competition 2021 with the *Silicon Valley* spec script - "I Want Your UX". He lives in St. Louis with his wife, son, and two dogs.

Benjamin Sawyer

is an independent comic artist, entertainment designer, and teacher. He loves video games, motorcycles, and fitness. Check out his work at www.sketchsawyer.com.

Elizabeth Schweitzer

is a longtime Ink & Drink contributor, hearkening back to the days of yore and Cicero's. She does law junk for the Man and Monies and does comics junk to remind her of her youth (and to justify buying expensive Bristol board and fancy inking pens at art supply stores). In her spare time she reads too many travel blogs and caters to her two mafioso-wannabe cats, Sonny and Fredo.

Kevin Taylor

is currently a PhD student and independent artist. He is also a veteran video games developer who has worked on eight titles for publishers including Bethesda Softworks, SEGA, Activision, Konami and Ubisoft. He remains passionate about engaging users in traditional and innovative means of storytelling. Follow his work on Instagram @Vindicator_9 and @Imperator_Interactive.

Thomas Watson

dabbles in multiple art mediums ranging from oil paint to digital. His paintings of late look into re-imagining mythological stories from different perspectives. With practice, Tom hopes to improve in comics and storytelling and make his own mythological worlds and stories in the future. Find him on Instagram @tommytsunami42.

Patrick Weck

works for the St. Louis Zoo, making and repairing fake things and sometimes painting murals. When he withdraws to his studio, the unearthly muse consumes him. Eldritch arthropods and prehistoric beasts pour forth from his pen or brush in mad rivulets like some primordial streamlet of the Mesozoic. Basically he enjoys drawing dinosaurs and aliens. He often collaborates with writer Nathan Kenkel, and recently illustrated the cover of his sci-fi novella *Exogeny*. Find him on Instagram @bluemaskart and online at PatrickWeck.artstation.com.

Joe Wills's

love for comics sparked after seeing a young Rob Liefeld in a Levi's Jeans commercial in 1991. He began drawing and creating stories at a young age, but it wasn't until adulthood that the passion for creating comics and an opportunity came to together with his first 3 pages published in Ink and Drink's fantasy anthology *Hammered*. He has contributed multiple times in various anthologies with Ink and Drink Comics. *Supreme Team*, published by Stache Publishing, was his first non-anthology book. During his career, he has worked on various projects behind the scenes, with very few credited works. He is currently working on a creator-owned book.

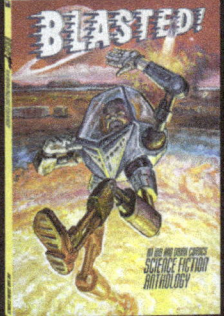

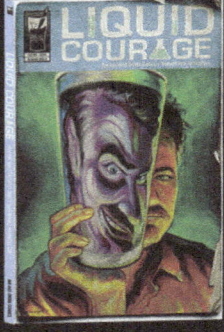

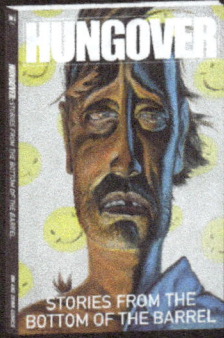

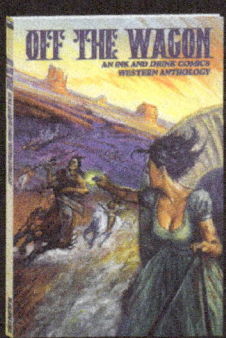

OFF THE WAGON
76 pages
Black and White
Western
April 2012

HAMMERED
90 pages
Black and White
Fantasy
October 2012

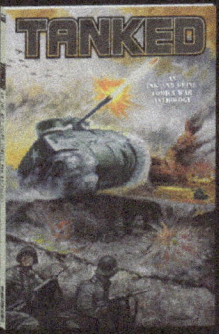

TANKED
96 pages
Black and White
War
April 2013

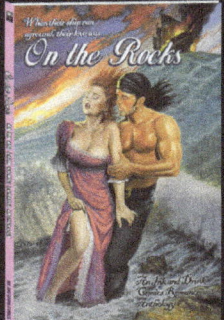

ON THE ROCKS
106 pages
Black and White
Romance
October 2013

SPIRITS OF ST. LOUIS II
Mad Zombie or Zombie Sacagawea cover
124 pages
Full Color
Horror
April 2016

CHASER
100 pages
Full Color
Crime
April 2017

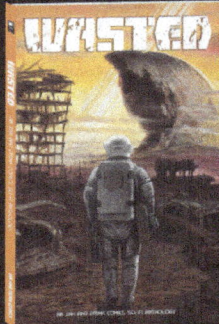

WASTED
120 pages
Full Color
Science Fiction
October 2017

DRY COUNTY
108 pages
Full Color
Western
October 2018

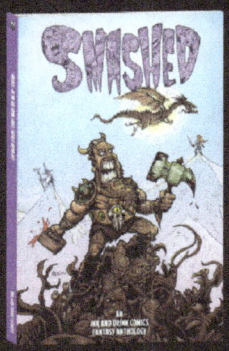

SMASHED
100 pages
Full Color
Fantasy
October 2018

BOMBED
84 pages
Full Color
War
April 2019

MIXER
84 pages
Full Color
Romance
April 2020

KYLE T.A.M.

www.ingramcontent.com/pod-product-compliance
Lightning Source LLC
Chambersburg PA
CBHW082033170626
46817CB00010B/3147